JUN 2001

AUBURN-PLACER COUNTY LIBRARY

AUBURN

P9-BYN-686

Auburn - Placer County Library
350 Nevada Street
Auburn, CA 95603

The Hungriest Boy in the World

The Hungriest Boy in the World

BY *Lensey Namioka*

ILLUSTRATED BY
Aki Sogabe

Holiday House / New York

To Shigeo
and Masako
L. N.

For my gluttonous son,
Steve
A. S.

Text copyright © 2001 by Lensey Namioka
Illustrations copyright © 2001 by Aki Sogabe
All Rights Reserved
Printed in the United States of America
www.holidayhouse.com
First Edition
The text typeface is Garamond #3.
The artwork was created with cut paper, watercolor, and airbrush.

Library of Congress Cataloging-in-Publication Data
Namioka, Lensey.
The hungriest boy in the world / by Lensey Namioka; illustrated by Aki Sogabe.—1st ed.
p. cm.
Summary: After swallowing the Hunger Monster, Jiro begins eating everything in sight,
until his family finds a way to lure the monster out of Jiro's stomach.
ISBN 0-8234-1542-2 (hardcover)
[1. Hunger—Fiction. 2. Japan—Fiction.] I. Sogabe, Aki, ill. II. Title.
PZ7.N1426 Hu 2001
{E}—dc21
00-025142

ONCE THERE WAS A JAPANESE BOY called
Jiro who lived with his family in a fishing village near
the Inland Sea. Jiro had one bad habit: he liked to put
things in his mouth.

If he found a strip of seaweed, he would put it in his
mouth to chew.

If he found a seashell, he would put it in his mouth
to taste the salt.

If he found a smooth pebble, he would put it in his
mouth to roll around.

One day, Jiro saw a purple blob on the ground.
Of course he picked it up and put it in his mouth.
   It moved.
   "Aaarrgh!" he cried. Before he could spit it out,
the blob went straight down his throat.
   Jiro had swallowed the Hunger Monster!

That night, Jiro's mother served sushi. She cooked rice, formed it into balls, and put a slice of fresh fish on top of each ball.

Jiro and his father and his brother, Taro, ate first. When they finished, his mother and his sister, Ohana, began to eat. Taro went outside, but Jiro stayed near the table.

I need more food! the Hunger Monster whispered to him.

"What do you want, Jiro?" asked his mother.

"I'm still hungry," he said.

"Still hungry!" cried his mother. "But I made enough sushi for everyone to get a big helping!"

"He ate all of his and even took a piece from Taro," said Ohana, who noticed such things.

Jiro's mother stared at him. "Well, you're growing. All right, you may have two of my pieces."

His mother held a piece out to him. His teeth chomped down so hard that she had to tug her chopsticks to free them.

She put the second piece on a plate and offered it to him gingerly. *Whoosh,* the piece of sushi disappeared. Ohana hunched protectively over her sushi.

"That's enough!" said his mother. "Go outside and play."

Jiro went outside. *I need more food!* said the Hunger
Monster. Jiro saw a bucket of fish guts. He put them to
his mouth and gulped them down.

But he was still hungry.

"Help me hang the nets, Jiro!" Taro shouted.

Jiro went over to the nets. They looked like noodles,
delicious noodles, seasoned with soy sauce.

"Hurry up, Jiro!" said Taro.

Jiro didn't answer. Taro looked around. Jiro was standing there with fish net hanging from his mouth, like someone slurping a bowl of ramen noodles.

Taro pulled the net from Jiro's mouth. "You chewed up the net! There's a big hole here!"

Jiro swallowed the bits of net he had been chewing, and the Hunger Monster took a rest...for a while.

In the middle of the night, the Hunger Monster began again. *I need more food!*

Jiro put his quilt to his mouth. Soon he found himself chewing and chewing. He was awakened the next morning by a scream. "Look at Jiro!" cried Ohana. "He's eaten half his quilt!"

She was exaggerating. Jiro had eaten only one quarter. The raw edge of the quilt, with cotton coming out, was still in his mouth.

"Oh, the poor boy!" said his mother. "I should have given him more sushi yesterday!"

"The bucket of fish guts is empty," said Ohana, who noticed such things. "Jiro ate them all up."

"Jiro was chewing on the fish nets," said Taro. "He ate some of them."

Everyone turned and stared at Jiro.

"Why are you eating so much, Jiro?" asked his father.

"I'm hungry," Jiro said.

"I'd better make breakfast right away," his mother said.

She hurried, but the rice took a long time to cook. *I need more food!* said the Monster.

Finally Jiro's mother set the table and arranged the cushions around the table. One of them was missing.

"Jiro ate one of the cushions," said Ohana. Jiro swallowed and burped.

"Something is definitely wrong with the boy," said his father. "I'd better get a doctor right away."

The doctor came with a big box of medicines. He felt Jiro's various pulses. "I'll prepare some medicine for him," he pronounced finally.

When the doctor turned to his medicine box, it was empty. Jiro was wiping some yellow powder from his lips.

"You ate all the medicines?" screamed the doctor. "You'll get sick!"

Jiro didn't get sick, because the Hunger Monster had eaten all the medicines. "I'm still hungry," he said.

The doctor turned pale. Wordlessly, he picked up his empty box of medicines, slung it over his shoulders, and tottered from the house.

"There's nothing the matter with the boy's health,"
said Jiro's father. "No, something else is wrong."

"Maybe he's under a magic spell," said Taro.

Jiro's father decided to take him to the village priest
and have him recite a prayer to undo the magic spell.

Packing three of his largest fish in a basket, Jiro's
father took him to the nearby temple. When they
arrived, only one fish was left. As Jiro picked the fish
bones out of his teeth, his father presented the fish to
the priest and explained his son's problem.

"Don't worry," said the priest. He tapped a bronze bowl softly with a stick, cleared his throat, and began to recite a prayer.

I need more food! said the Hunger Monster. The priest's chanting was interrupted by the sound of *ping, ping, ping*. His beads were bouncing on the floor. Jiro had chewed through their string and was popping them into his mouth.

The priest jumped up, quivering with fury. Terribly embarrassed, Jiro's father dragged his son home from the temple.

"We'd better consult a medium," he said when he got home. "A medium can communicate with the supernatural and tell us what's wrong."

He packed some more of his fish—the supply had gone down—and set off with Jiro for the home of the village medium.

The medium was a middle-aged woman with long, gray hair. She lit some incense and worked herself into a trance. Soon she began to speak in a strange, deep voice. "I'm the Hunger Monster inside Jiro. I need food!"

When the medium woke up from her trance, her voice was soft and gentle again. She patted Jiro on the head. "What a sweet little boy...Ow!" She backed away and pulled strands of her hair from Jiro's mouth.

Back home, Jiro's father told his family what the medium had said. "Apparently Jiro has swallowed the Hunger Monster."

"We must get the Hunger Monster to come out," said Taro.

"The Hunger Monster won't come out unless there's someone else it can enter," said Ohana.

The family tried to think of a solution.

Taro had an idea. "Let's get a puppet master from Awaji!"

Jiro's family spent all day preparing a feast. When the food was set out, Jiro was tied to a pillar behind the table. Taro came into the house and whispered, "The puppet master is here."

The puppet master stayed out of sight, but he placed his puppet in front of the table. The puppet was about the same height as Jiro, and she had the face of a beautiful young woman. Bowing politely to the family, the puppet said, "How kind of you to invite me to your feast. I love to eat, and I can hardly wait to start."

Jiro's father bowed back. "Our food is poor, but we are honored by your presence. Please don't hold back."

The puppet moved to the table. "Oh, my goodness!" she crooned. "These are all my favorites!"

As the puppet bent over the food, Jiro began to struggle. Taro had to add another rope to hold him fast to the pillar.

The puppet began to make slobbering sounds. "Oh, how delicious is this octopus! How sweet are these clams! How creamy is this omelet!"

Jiro began to feel a furious
wobbling in his stomach. Then
something zipped up his gullet.
He quickly opened his mouth
wide. Opposite him, the puppet
opened her mouth even wider.

Something shot out of Jiro's mouth and flew straight into the puppet's mouth. Since the puppet's body was just empty space enclosed by cloth, the Hunger Monster fell *clunk* to the floor.

Taro stood ready, holding a broom in his hands, and swept the Hunger Monster out the door.

Everybody cheered. Jiro's father thanked the puppet
master. "It was a wonderful performance!"

"Can we eat now?" Jiro asked. "I'm hungry!"

They all turned and stared at him.

Jiro laughed. "I'm joking!"

They celebrated by sitting down to the delicious feast.
Ohana saw that Jiro ate no more than his share. She
noticed such things.

What about the Hunger Monster? It was outside, waiting for someone else to pick it up and put it in his mouth.